GET THE GIGGLES WITH

YUCK

by Matt and Dave

Join Yuck's fanclub at
YUCKWEB.COM

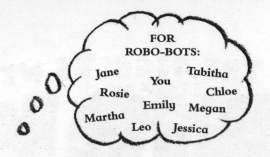

FOR
ROBO-BOTS:

Jane   You   Tabitha
Rosie   Chloe
        Emily   Megan
Martha
    Leo   Jessica

SIMON AND SCHUSTER

First published in Great Britain in 2009
by Simon & Schuster UK Ltd
A CBS COMPANY
1st Floor, 222 Gray's Inn Road, London WC1X 8HB

1 3 5 7 9 10 8 6 4 2

A CIP catalogue record for this book is
available from the British Library

ISBN 978-1-84738-299-3

Printed and bound in Great Britain by
Cox & Wyman Ltd Reading Berkshire

www.simonandschuster.co.uk
www.yuckweb.com

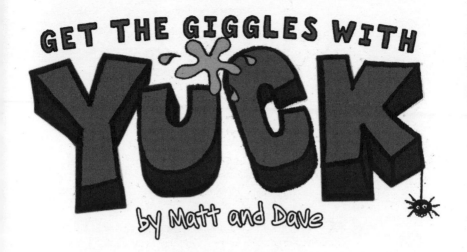

GET THE GIGGLES WITH

YUCK

by Matt and Dave

YUCK'S ROBOTIC BOTTOM

AND

YUCK'S WILD WEEKEND

Illustrated by Nigel Baines

YUCK'S ROBOTIC BOTTOM

Yuck dangled a long piece of string from his bedroom window to the garden below. The string was covered with sticky, red, strawberry jam.

He watched excitedly as ants began crawling up the string eating the jam. They crawled in a line, one after the other, all the way up to a jar on Yuck's windowsill.

Yuck smiled. His invention worked!

Earlier that day, Yuck had been on a school trip to the science museum to see an exhibition about world-famous inventions, and his homework was to make an invention of his own. Yuck had invented his very own ant catcher!

He glanced down and saw his sister, Polly Princess, step into the garden. Attached to her shoes were two paper plates on drinking straws.

"Why are you wearing those?" Yuck called to her.

Polly looked up. "They're my invention," she told him. "They're umbrellas that keep my shoes dry in the rain. I call them shumbrellas."

"DUMBrellas more like," Yuck said giggling. "What a silly invention."

Polly scowled at Yuck. "You're just jealous because my invention's better than yours." She looked at the piece of string dangling from Yuck's window. "What's this for, anyway?" she said, tugging it.

"Hey, hands off my ant catcher!"

"Aaargh!" Polly cried as ants showered

 down onto her. She shook her head and pulled at her hair trying to get them out. "I'm telling on you!"

She stormed indoors and a moment later Mum stepped out.

"Yuck, come downstairs at once!" Mum called.

"But, Mum—"

"No buts, Yuck.
Come down NOW!"

Yuck went downstairs to
the kitchen and found Mum
picking ants from Polly's
hair. "Yuck, why did you
throw ants on your sister?" Mum asked.

"I didn't," Yuck told her. "She did it
herself. She was trying to ruin my invention."

Polly glared at Yuck. "An ant catcher's
not a proper invention," she said. "It's
disgusting."

"Polly's right, Yuck," Mum told him.
"You'll have to invent something else."

While Mum finished picking the ants
from Polly's hair, Yuck
sneaked to the kitchen
cupboard and took
out a packet of
chocolate cake mix.
He headed back
upstairs and set to
work on another yucky invention.

Using his baseball cap as a mixing bowl, Yuck shook in the chocolate cake mix, then fetched a tube of glue from his model-making box. He squeezed the glue into the

hat and stirred it with the cake mix, making a sticky brown goo. Perfect, Yuck thought. He was inventing the world's stickiest fake dog poo!

He scooped out a handful then stepped to his window. Polly Princess was back in the garden watering her shumbrellas with a watering can, testing to see if they worked. Yuck threw the dog poo onto the garden path behind her. "I bet it's difficult to walk in those," he called down.

Polly turned round. "It's easy." She walked down the path and stepped straight into the dog poo. "Uurgh!"

Polly tried to lift her foot but it was stuck. "Help! My shoe! My shoe's stuck in a poo!"

Mum came running out of the back door. "What's the matter, Polly?"

"Sticky dog poo!" Polly shrieked.

"Dog poo?" Mum asked, confused. "But we haven't got a dog."

Mum glanced up at Yuck's window as he ducked back into his room giggling.

Rockits! Yuck thought. Inventions are fun!

Yuck sneaked into Polly's room and borrowed her Bubble-Fun Bubble Maker from her toy box. It was time for another yucky invention. He put the Bubble Maker on his bedroom floor and opened its lid where the bubble mixture went. He filled it with yucky ingredients: half a glass of curdled milk, a mouldy banana and a lump of pongy cheese from an old sandwich. Then he took off his smelly socks and stuffed those in too, along with a pair of whiffy underpants. Yuck flicked the switch on the Bubble Maker and it began rumbling as bubbles started coming out. He was inventing a stink machine!

At that moment, his door burst open and Polly hopped in wearing only one shoe. "YOU put that sticky poo on the path, didn't you?" she said.

"Polly, can't you see I'm busy inventing?" Yuck told her.

Polly saw bubbles floating around Yuck's room. She saw her Bubble Maker on the floor. "Hey, that's mine!"

"I've turned it into a stink machine. Do you like it?"

A bubble burst in Polly's face. "PHWOAR!" she cried, pinching her nose. It stank of pongy cheese. More bubbles burst around her, each letting off a different stink: curdled milk… smelly socks… mouldy banana… whiffy underpants…

"Mum!" Polly called. "Yuck's being disgusting again!"

Mum came running upstairs to Yuck's room and saw the bubbles bursting. She saw the baseball cap loaded with sticky dog poo, and the jam jar on his windowsill full of ants. "Yuck, get rid of these revolting inventions right now!" she yelled.

"But Mum, they're for my homework," Yuck told her.

"These aren't proper inventions," Polly said, choking on a big bubble that stank of whiffy underpants. "They're gross."

"Polly's right, Yuck," Mum said. "You're not to invent anything else yucky!"

Mum and Polly left Yuck's room and went downstairs coughing.

Yuck decided that when he was EMPEROR OF EVERYTHING, he'd invent all kinds of yucky things: slime-squirting spyplanes, burp-blasting tanks, and even a sewage submarine. If Polly tried to stop him, his inventions would launch an ATTACK!

Yuck stashed his yucky inventions under his bed, then tried to think what else he could make. He remembered the inventions at the science museum: the radio... the electric light bulb... the television... the computer... the robot... Suddenly, Yuck's eyes lit up with excitement! A ROBOT! he thought. He could have LOTS of fun with a robot. If only he knew how to make one...

That night, Yuck was lying in bed thinking how he could invent a robot when he had a brilliant idea. While everyone was asleep, he crept downstairs to the garden and searched in Dad's shed. He found some old cardboard boxes and carried them

indoors. From the hall cupboard, he fetched
some shiny coloured wrapping paper, a roll
of sticky tape and a stack of gift labels. He
wrapped the boxes in the shiny paper and
stuck a label to each with a hand-written
message. Finally, he
placed them outside
the front door to
make it look like
they'd been delivered
by the postman.

In the morning, he woke up hearing
Mum calling up the stairs. "Yuck, there are
some parcels here for you!"

Yuck quickly dressed and raced down to
see. "Parcels? I wonder who they could be
from?" he said innocently.

Polly came downstairs to see what was
happening. "Why has Yuck got parcels?"
she asked.

On the front door step were the boxes
in shiny paper just as he'd left them the
night before.

Polly pushed past him and snatched one of them. She read its label: "To Professor  Yuck, from NASA Space Research. **TOP SECRET**"

She looked at Yuck. "It says Professor. You're not a Professor."

She checked the labels on other parcels.

"To Professor Yuck, from Robotico Research. **TOP SECRET**

To Professor Yuck, from Inventors Inc. **TOP SECRET**."

Yuck smiled. "Oh, these must be the top-secret scientific parts I've been waiting for."

"Top-secret scientific parts?"

"For my new invention."

"What invention?" Polly asked.

"A robot!" Yuck told her. "I'm inventing a walking, talking, remote-controlled robot."

"Hey, that's not fair," Polly said jealously. She watched as Yuck picked up the parcels, balancing them one on top of the other, and stepped out of the door.

"I'll see you at school," he said smiling. But for his robot plan to work, Yuck would need a friend to help him. And he knew just the person to ask.

At the school gates,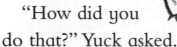
Yuck saw his friend
Little Eric shaking
people's hands as
they arrived. Each
person yelped and
leapt into the air.

"How did you
do that?" Yuck asked.

Little Eric showed Yuck a metal buzzer
in his hand.

"Is that your invention?"

"It's a Buzz-o-laff," Little Eric whispered.
"I got it free with *KLUNK* magazine." He
stared up at Yuck's stack of parcels. "What
are you doing with those?"

"I'm inventing a robot," Yuck told him.
"Come on. You can help."

They needed a place where no one
would see them so they sneaked to the
school toilets. Yuck put the parcels down.

"What's in them?" Little Eric asked.

"Nothing," Yuck giggled. "Watch this."

Yuck tore a hole in either end of one of the parcels and slid it onto Little Eric's arm. Then he made holes in another parcel and slid it onto Little Eric's leg. One after the other, Yuck slid all the parcels onto Little Eric, completely covering his body. He put the last parcel over Little Eric's head. With a felt-tipped pen he drew on buttons, dials, nuts  and bolts. He drew on a robot mouth and robot ears, then pulled off the gift labels and tore a small slit for Little Eric to see through. Finally, he fetched ten toilet-roll tubes and slid them onto Little Eric's fingers. "Finished," he said.

Little Eric stepped out of the cubicle and looked in the mirror. "Brilliant!" he said. He looked just like a robot!

"Try talking like a robot," Yuck told him.

"**BLEEP, BLIP, BLOOP,**" Little Eric replied, speaking in a robot voice.

"Perfect," Yuck said. From his bag, he took a remote control. It was the one for

the TV at home. "I'll pretend
to control you with this."
Yuck pointed the remote
control at Little Eric and pressed a button.
Little Eric started walking like a robot.

"Don't let anyone know it's you," Yuck
said, and they headed to class.

Yuck peered through the classroom door
and saw Mrs Wagon the Dragon taking the
register. Everyone was sitting at their desks
with their inventions. Schoolie Julie had
invented a fan to stop ice cream melting
in the sun. Fartin Martin and Tom Bum
had invented rocket
pants to help them
run faster. Kate the
Skate had invented a
bendy skateboard for
skating round corners.

As Yuck crept
in, the Dragon
grabbed him:
"You're late, Yuck!"

"Sorry, Miss, I've been finishing my invention," Yuck said.

"Oh, yes? And what have you invented?" the Dragon asked.

"A robot," Yuck told her.

The Dragon raised her glasses and stared at Yuck in astonishment. "A robot?"

"That's right." Yuck pointed his remote control towards the door. He pressed a button and in stepped Little Eric dressed in the robot costume.

The class gasped. "Wow! A real robot!"

"**BLEEP, BLIP, BLOOP,**" the robot said, marching towards the Dragon.

"It's a walking, talking, remote-controlled robot," Yuck explained.

"How remarkable!" the Dragon said, inspecting it. "You invented this all by yourself?"

The robot held out its hand to the Dragon. "**BLOOP, BLEEP, BLIP.** Pleased to meet you," it said.

As the Dragon shook the robot's hand, she leapt in the air. "Aaaargh!" she yelped.

"Oh, dear. You must have got an electric shock," Yuck told her.

The robot was giggling. Little Eric had the Buzz-o-laff strapped to his hand.

Aaaargh!

Yuck pointed his remote control and directed the robot to an empty seat at the back of the class. He sat beside it. "We fooled her," he whispered.

The Dragon's hair was standing on end from the Buzz-o-laff. She looked at the register. "Does anyone know where Little Eric is today?" she asked.

Megan the Mouth put her hand up. "He was at the school gates this morning, Miss."

The robot put its hand up. "**BLEEP, BLIP, BLOOP**. He went home feeling ill," it said.

The Dragon looked at the robot, surprised to hear it answer.

Yuck quickly put his hand up. "Little Eric's definitely not here, Miss," he said.

The Dragon marked Little Eric as absent. "Well, I'm delighted to announce that Mrs Appliance from the science museum will be coming to school tomorrow to see your inventions. What's more, for the best invention in school, she'll be awarding two tickets to Space World."

"Space World! Fantastic!" everyone said.

Space World was a theme park with space rockets, space food and intergalactic rides. Yuck had always wanted to go there.

"I suggest you spend today making sure your inventions are in tip-top working order," the Dragon continued. She started walking among the desks, seeing what everyone had invented.

Inside the robot costume Little Eric's nose was twitching. The box on his head was dusty. "ATCHOO!"

Ben Bong turned round from the desk in front. "Did your robot just sneeze?" he asked Yuck.

Snot was leaking from the box on Little Eric's head. Yuck wiped it off and rubbed it between his fingers. "It's robot oil," he said.

Frank the Tank turned round to see. "Why's your robot wearing glasses?" he asked.

"Those aren't glasses, they're laser goggles," Yuck said.

"Laser goggles?"

Yuck pointed to a red button on the remote control. "If I press this button, its eyes fire laser beams – exterminator beams!"

Frank the Tank stared in awe at the robot. "How did you manage to build it?"

Yuck smiled. "It's easy when you're a brilliant inventor like me."

At breaktime, Yuck took his robot to the playground to have some fun. He pointed the control and pressed a button. The robot span round. He pressed another button and the robot jumped up and down. He pressed another button and the robot did a robot dance. Soon a crowd had gathered to watch. Polly Princess and her friend Juicy Lucy pushed to the front.

"Polly, how did Yuck invent a robot?" Juicy Lucy whispered, seeing the robot do a blip-bleep boogie.

"He should be disqualified," Polly replied. "He had top-secret scientific parts delivered this morning." She dashed to Yuck and snatched the remote control from his hand.

"Hey, give that back!" Yuck said.

Polly pressed a button trying to send the robot into the school pond. But the robot kept dancing. "It's broken," she said, shaking the control. She pressed all the buttons, trying to make the robot short-circuit.

"Not the red one!" Frank the Tank called.

The robot stopped dancing and began marching towards Polly. "Prepare laser beams. **BLEEP**," it said.

"Run, Polly! It's got exterminator beams!" Frank the Tank warned her.

"Exterminator beams?"

The robot stared straight at her. "**BLEEP, BLOOP, BLIP!** Exterminate Polly! Exterminate Polly!"

Polly began quivering.

"They melt you like butter," Yuck said.

Polly dropped the remote control and fled across the playground. Mr Reaper the headmaster came out to see what the noise was and Polly ran straight into him, knocking him to the ground.

"Mind where you're going!" the Reaper yelled.

"But, Sir. A robot's after me!" Polly said.

The Reaper stood up brushing his trousers. "A robot? What robot?" He looked across the playground and saw the robot standing beside Yuck. He came walking over. "Where did this robot come from, Yuck?" he asked.

"I invented it, Sir," Yuck replied.

"How remarkable! You invented a robot all by yourself?"

"Yes, Sir. It's a walking, talking, remote-controlled robot. Let me show you." Yuck pressed a button on the remote control and the robot headed off back into school. Yuck ran after it, leaving the Reaper amazed.

Yuck whispered to Little Eric: "We've fooled them all. Space World here we come!"

At lunchtime, Yuck and his robot sat in the school canteen with plates of sausages, beans and chips. Little Eric found it difficult to hold a fork with his toilet-roll fingers, and the robot head had no hole for its mouth.

"Let me help you," Yuck said, making a small tear in the cardboard. He posted a sausage through and Little Eric giggled.

"That went up my nose!"

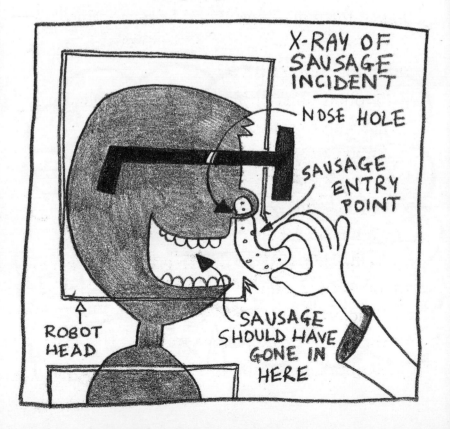

From a nearby table, Polly and Lucy were watching.

"Robots don't eat sausages," Lucy whispered.

They watched as the robot tried to eat its beans. Tomato sauce dribbled down its chin, then it let out a **BURP!**

"Robots don't burp either," Polly replied. "Yuck's up to something. I'm sure of it."

All lunchtime, they spied on Yuck and his robot. In the playground, they heard Yuck telling the robot a joke.

"What do robots eat for dinner?"

"**BLIP, BLEEP, BLOOP.** I don't know. What do robots eat for dinner?"

"Microchips!"

Yuck and the robot both laughed.

"Robot's don't laugh," Polly whispered.

Polly and Lucy crouched in the bushes, watching Yuck and the robot play football. The robot cheered when it scored: "Goal!"

"Robot's don't cheer, either," Lucy whispered.

A while later, Polly and Lucy saw Yuck and his robot go into the toilets.

"Robots definitely don't go to the toilet!" Polly said.

Polly and Lucy sneaked in after them. They saw Yuck go into one cubicle and his robot go into another. They crept to the cubicle with the robot in it and peered under the door. The robot was sliding parcels from its legs. Underneath, it was wearing trousers!

"That's not a robot!" Polly said.

Polly barged the
door open and saw
the robot sitting on
the toilet! She yanked its
head and a box came off
in her hands. "It's Little Eric!"
Polly and Lucy gasped.

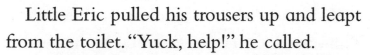

Little Eric pulled his trousers up and leapt
from the toilet. "Yuck, help!" he called.

"So this is what you've been up to!"
Polly said. "Well, now the game's up!" She
tore the boxes from Little Eric's arms and
legs, ripping them to pieces.

Yuck burst into the cubicle. "Leave Little
Eric alone!"

"Oh, dear, Yuck," Polly said smirking. "It
looks like your robot's broken now."

Little Eric was picking up pieces of
cardboard. Polly barged past him. "Come
on, Lucy. Let's go."

"Now what are we going to do?" Little
Eric said to Yuck. "Without the robot, we'll
never win the tickets to Space World."

That evening, Yuck decided he'd build a new robot costume. But when he looked in Dad's shed for more cardboard boxes, they'd all gone. He found Dad in the living room watching television. "Dad, what happened to the cardboard boxes in your shed?"

"Your sister took them," Dad replied.

Yuck raced upstairs and opened Polly's bedroom door. There, standing by her bed, was a new robot! It was Polly, dressed in a brand-new robot costume of her own!

"Hey, what do you think you're doing?" Yuck asked.

Polly laughed. "BLEEP, BLOOP, BLIP. If you tell, I'll exterminate you." She took off her robot head and glared at him. "It's Lucy and me who'll be going to Space World now!"

That night, Yuck lay in bed thinking what to do. Tomorrow, Mrs Appliance from the science museum would be coming to school. If he didn't find a way of stopping Polly, she'd win the prize for best invention.

At that moment, Yuck smelt a pong wafting from under his bed. He leaned down and saw his yucky inventions: the jar of ants, the hat of sticky dog poo and his stink machine. He had an idea!

Yuck hid the jar and the poo in his schoolbag, then carried the stink machine to Polly's room. She was snoring and her robot costume was laying on the floor. Yuck rummaged through it and opened one of

the boxes. He placed the stink machine inside, then took a cardboard tube and attached it to the box like an exhaust pipe. Tomorrow, Polly would be in for a surprise…

The next day at school, everyone gathered in the assembly hall with their inventions. Polly was wearing her robot costume and Lucy was beside her holding a remote control.

"Yuck, why don't we tell the Reaper what they're up to?" Little Eric whispered.

"Because I've got a plan," Yuck replied. He opened his bag and showed Little Eric

the jar of ants and the hat full of sticky dog poo. Then they crept behind Polly, and Yuck pointed to the back of her costume where the cardboard tube was poking from the robot's bottom. Yuck whispered something to Little Eric and Little Eric giggled.

They watched as Mrs Appliance from the science museum came in with the Reaper.

Mrs Appliance began inspecting each invention in turn. Schoolie Julie demonstrated her fan for cooling ice cream. But when she switched it on, the ice cream blew in her face.

Fartin Martin and Tom Bum showed Mrs Appliance their rocket pants for rocket-powered running. But when they turned on the gas, the pants blew up with a **BANG!**

Kate the Skate tried out her bendy skateboard for going round corners, but it span round and round in circles making her dizzy.

"I'm sorry about this," the Reaper said to Mrs Appliance. "I'm sure someone will have invented something that works."

Mrs Appliance inspected the inventions, but they were all useless. Finally she reached Juicy Lucy and her robot. "How remarkable," Mrs Appliance said. "A robot! Did you make this yourself?"

"I invented it with my friend Polly," Juicy Lucy explained.

The Reaper looked down at Lucy. "And where is Polly today?" he asked.

"She's not at school," Lucy lied. "I think she's ill." Lucy pressed a button on the remote control. Inside the costume, Polly moved her arm and the robot waved.

"How ingenious!" Mrs Appliance said.

Juicy Lucy pressed another button and the robot took a step forward.

"How incredible!" Mrs Appliance said.

Lucy pressed another button and the robot spoke: "**BLIP, BLEEP, BLOOP.** Hello."

"Genius! A walking, talking, remote-controlled robot!" Mrs Appliance said. "This is by far the best invention in the school."

Yuck stepped behind the robot and sneakily reached into the box on its bottom. He flicked the switch on his stink machine inside, and the robot's bottom started rumbling. A bubble leaked from the cardboard tube and burst, letting off a stinky gas.

"Phwoar!" Mrs Appliance said. "What's that awful smell?"

"It stinks!" the Reaper added, waving his arms to clear the air.

Yuck peered round from behind the robot. "I think the robot's malfunctioning," he said.

Little Eric pointed to the robot's bottom.
More bubbles were coming out of it. "It
seems to be blowing off!"

Yuck and Little Eric giggled as bubbles
floated from the robot's bottom and burst
in the air.

"Phwoargh!
What a stink!"
Lucy said. The
bubbles smelt
like whiffy
underpants.

While everyone was coughing and choking, Yuck reached into his bag and grabbed his jar of ants. Sneakily, he poured them into the box at the back of the robot.

The robot started twitching. "Eek, **BLEEP**, ooo!" it said. It began hopping from one leg to the other. Inside the robot costume, ants were crawling up and down Polly's legs. They were biting her. "**BLIP**, argh! **BLOOP**, ouch!"

"Why is this robot behaving so oddly?" Mrs Appliance asked Lucy.

"I've no idea," Lucy replied.

The robot was hopping and screaming. "Ow! **BLOOP!** Argh!" It started running through the assembly hall, barging past the other children, knocking into their inventions. Its bottom was firing out bubbles: streams of them, one after the other, bursting with pongy smells.

"Stop that robot!" the Reaper cried.

All the children were pinching their
noses. "It stinks!"

Bubbles were bursting everywhere.
They smelt of curdled milk, smelly socks,
mouldy banana, pongy cheese and
whiffy underpants.

"**PHWOAR!**" everyone cried.

"Lucy, make it stop!"
the Reaper ordered.

"But I can't!" Lucy said, chasing the
robot. She was pointing the remote control,
frantically pressing buttons. "Stop!" she
cried. "Stop!"

But the robot was out of control.

Yuck stepped beside Mrs Appliance. "Leave this to me!" he said. From his bag, he took out a lump of sticky brown goo.

"What's that?" Mrs Appliance asked him.

"This is one of my inventions," Yuck replied. "It's the world's stickiest dog poo." He threw the poo across the assembly hall and it splatted in the robot's path.

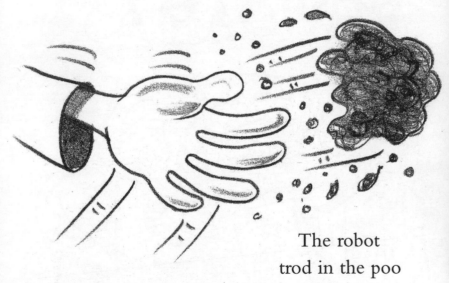

The robot trod in the poo and its foot stuck to the floor. "**BLEEEEP!** I'm stuck!" it cried.

"What a brilliant invention," Mrs Appliance said to Yuck.

She ran to the robot, that was now coughing and struggling. "Get me out of here! Get me out of here!" it shouted.

"This isn't a real robot!" the Reaper said, walking towards it. "There's someone in here!" The Reaper yanked off the robot's head...

"Polly!" the Reaper said angrily.
"What a cheat! You and Lucy are in
BIG TROUBLE."

Polly's face was crawling with ants.
"HELP!" she screamed. **"GET THEM OFF ME!"**

Yuck stepped forward. "Leave this to me," he said. From his bag he took out a jam jar and a length of string covered in jam. He laid the string on the ground and the ants began crawling along it, away from Polly, back towards the jar.

Mrs Appliance stared in astonishment as Yuck gathered all the ants back up. "How brilliant!" she exclaimed.

"This is my ant catcher," Yuck told her. "It's another of my inventions."

"Help me!" Polly coughed.
"Help me!" She was surrounded
by bursting bubbles, choking on
the stench. The robot's bottom was still
blowing off. "Make it stop!"

"Leave this to me," Yuck said again. He slid the cardboard box from the robot's bottom, then reached in and turned off his stink machine. The bubbles stopped.

"How did you do that?" Mrs Appliance asked.

"This is my invention too," Yuck told her.

Mrs Appliance stared in astonishment at the box with the cardboard tube poking from it. "This is incredible!" she said. "I've never seen anything like it. Do you realise what you've invented? This is the world's first robotic bottom!"

She took two tickets from her pocket and gave them to Yuck. "Here you are. I award you the prize for the best invention in school: two tickets to Space World."

Yuck smiled and handed a ticket to Little Eric. "Space World here we come!"

YUCK'S WILD WEEKEND

A hairy hand with long nails reached over Yuck's shoulder. He glanced round. Little Eric was wearing his Hairy-Bear Beast Glove, making the sign of THE CLAW.

"**GRRRR**... Are we ready to explore the wild?" Little Eric asked.

Yuck held his hand up, returning the secret sign. "**GRRRR**... The equipment is prepared."

On Yuck's bed was a backpack and a
pile of survival equipment: a tent, sleeping
bags, a torch, a compass, a catapult, snow-
shoes, a fishing rod, a net and a rope.

"What about the food rations?" Little
Eric asked.

By Yuck's feet lay two empty
Chocoblock wrappers. "We've eaten them,"
he said. "We'll just have to survive on what
we can find." He was holding a book called

How to Survive in The Wild. It was written
by Bushtucker Bill and was full of ways
to survive in wild places: in the jungle,
on a mountain, in the desert and even in
a snowstorm.

Yuck and Little Eric loaded the
equipment into the backpack, then put on
hats that they'd camouflaged with lettuce
leaves. They grabbed the fishing rod, net and
rope, and ran downstairs.

Mum was in the kitchen clearing the plates from lunch. "So that's where my lettuce went," she said, seeing Yuck and Little Eric's hats as they crept past. "You're meant to eat your salad, Yuck, not wear it."

"But this is camouflage, Mum," Yuck told her. "We're off to the wild!"

Yuck opened the back door and ran outside.

"Be good," Mum called.

Yuck and Little Eric were off on a wild weekend! They were going camping in the garden. They raced across the lawn and stopped under a tall tree.

Yuck placed the backpack on the ground. "We'll pitch our tent here," he said.

But just then, Yuck's sister, Polly Princess, called from the house: "Oh, no you won't!" She came running down the garden towards them. She was wearing a backpack too! Little Eric's sister, Juicy Lucy, was with her, carrying a yellow blanket.

Polly raced to Yuck. "What do you think you're doing?" she asked.

"You know what we're doing. We're camping in the garden," Yuck told her.

"Oh, no you're not. Lucy and I are camping in the garden this weekend."

"But you said you were going to the cinema," Yuck replied.

Polly grinned. "We've changed our minds."

"You won't like it in the wild," Yuck told Polly. "There are dangerous animals and sinking swamps and—"

"You need specialist survival equipment," Little Eric added. He was holding the net and rope and fishing rod.

"Nonsense," Polly said. She snatched Yuck's backpack and threw it in the bushes.

"Hey, why did you do that?"

Dad looked over from his vegetable patch. "Play nicely," he called. "There's plenty of room for all of you."

Polly barged Yuck out of the way and started unpacking her kit: sun cream... sunglasses... a radio... magazines...

Lucy laid the yellow blanket on the ground. "Now go away. We were here first," she sneered.

"Come on, Eric. We'll find somewhere better to camp," Yuck said, pulling his backpack from the bushes. He headed to the other side of the garden by the fence.

"Why do they always have to ruin everything?" Little Eric said. "They're only camping because we are."

Yuck decided that when he was EMPEROR OF EVERYTHING, he'd live in a big tent in a wild forest full of beasts. If Polly tried to come camping, he'd send the beasts to GOBBLE HER UP.

As Yuck and Little Eric started putting their tent up, a breeze wafted across the garden towards Polly and Lucy.

"Phwoar!" Polly called. "Your tent stinks!"

Yuck's tent was still damp from the last time he'd been camping and had packed it away wet with rain. It had mould and fungus growing on it and smelt like a compost heap.

Yuck saw Polly pinching her nose. "It
serves you right for stealing our place," he
called to her. Polly and Lucy were putting
their tent up under the tree. It was pink
with purple spots.

"Their tent looks like it's got measles,"
Little Eric said giggling.

"I've got an idea," Yuck whispered.
"Watch this."

Yuck crept to the vegetable patch where
Dad was busy planting seeds. Sneakily, he
gathered a handful of long juicy worms,
then ran behind the tree by Polly and
Lucy's tent. He reached out, laying the
worms among their tent pegs.

Polly reached for a peg. "Eeek!" she
cried, as a worm wriggled in her fingers.

"Urrgh!" Lucy
screamed, seeing it
wrap around
Polly's hand.

Dad looked over.
"What's wrong,
Polly?" he called.

"It's revolting!"
Polly shrieked.
"There are worms
in our tent pegs!"

Yuck was giggling.

As he raced back to Little Eric. Polly
shouted: "Just you wait, Yuck! I'll get you
for this!"

When their camp was ready, Yuck and Little Eric set off to explore the wild. They streaked mud on their faces and lay face downwards, crawling across the lawn, pretending they were on a jungle safari.

"Keep your eyes peeled," Yuck whispered. "There's danger in the jungle, remember."

Little Eric was following a trail of slime. "Look, there's a jungle slime beast!" he said, pointing to a slug.

"And there's a man-eating spider!" Yuck said, pointing to a spider's web on a bush. A hairy garden spider was crawling across it.

Just then, a tennis ball flew over and smacked Yuck on the head. "Ow!" He looked across the garden and saw Polly standing by her tent holding a tennis racket.

"Oops!" Polly called. "Did I accidentally hit you with my ball?"

"Leave us alone, Polly," Yuck called back. "We're exploring the jungle."

Polly was laughing at them. "Don't be silly. This isn't the jungle. It's the garden."

"And you both look stupid," Lucy added.

Polly and Lucy ducked inside their tent sniggering.

"Look what they've done," Little Eric said. He pointed to the spider's web. Polly's ball had gone right through it and the spider was now hanging by a thread.

"Let's teach them
a lesson," Yuck
whispered. He cupped
the spider in his hand,
then sneaked across the
garden and placed it at
the entrance to Polly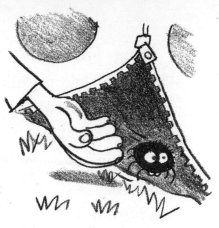
and Lucy's tent. The spider crawled inside.

Little Eric ran over with a handful of
slug slime and they hid behind the tree.

In the tent, Polly was whispering to
Lucy: "They're not explorers. They're just
naughty boys."

"I wish they'd go indoors," Lucy said.
"Then we'd have the garden to ourselves."

Just then, Polly felt something crawling
up her leg. It was scuttling up inside her
trousers. "Aaargh!" she screamed, leaping

from the tent.

Little Eric threw
the slug slime onto
the blanket and Polly
slipped over. "Urgh!"

Lucy poked her head out. "Are you okay, Polly?"

Polly was sliding on the slug slime. "Something's crawling in my trousers!"

Dad rushed over. "What's wrong, Polly?"

Polly was frantically shaking her leg. "Get it off me!"

A spider crawled out and Dad picked it up. "It's just a friendly garden spider," he said. "It's perfectly harmless, Polly." He carried it to the bushes then went back to his gardening.

Polly saw Yuck and Little Eric giggling by the tree. "That was you two, wasn't it? I'll get you back!"

Yuck and Little Eric quickly raced across the garden. "That'll teach her to mess with explorers," Little Eric laughed.

They ducked into their tent, and searched among their survival equipment preparing for another expedition. "Let's put on our snow shoes and explore the arctic," Yuck said.

From the backpack he pulled out two old tennis rackets and tied them to his trainers. Little Eric tied two old table tennis bats to his. They walked side by side across the lawn pretending they were tramping through deep snow.

"Which way to the North Pole?" Little Eric asked.

Yuck checked his compass. "That way," he said, pointing along the fence.

They pretended they were struggling through a snowy blizzard.

"It's c-c-cold here," Yuck said, his teeth chattering.

Little Eric pretended to shiver. "We have to k-keep g-going."

At that moment, a frisbee flew over and whacked Little Eric on the head. He turned and saw Polly and Lucy giggling.

"Why are you wearing those things on your feet?" Lucy called.

"These are snow shoes," Little Eric called back. "We're exploring the arctic."

Lucy laughed. "Don't be silly. This isn't the arctic. It's the garden."

"And you both look stupid," Polly added.

Polly and Lucy were laying on their blanket trying to sunbathe.

Yuck whispered in Little Eric's ear: "Let's see how they deal with an arctic snowstorm."

Yuck and Little Eric took off their snow shoes then crept to the tree by Polly and Lucy's tent. They climbed up it and crawled along a branch. Yuck looked down through the leaves. He scratched his head, and Little Eric did the same. Large flakes of white dandruff began falling down onto Polly and Lucy.

"Hey, it's snowing," Lucy said, confused.

Polly sat up. "It can't be. It's summertime."

Lucy poked her tongue out to catch a snowflake.

Polly looked up and saw Yuck and Little
Eric in the tree above, scratching their
heads. "Urgh, this isn't snow! It's dandruff!"

Lucy looked up. "That's revolting!" she said, spitting the dandruff from her mouth.

Yuck and Little Eric climbed down and raced across the garden. They dived into their tent, rolling around with laughter.

Yuck told Little Eric a joke: "What do snowmen eat for breakfast?"

"I don't know, what do snowmen eat for breakfast?"

"Snowflakes!"

Just then, their tent collapsed, covering them in a bundle of mouldy cloth. "Hey, what's going on?" Little Eric asked.

They could hear footsteps outside. Little Eric fumbled for the zip, then poked his head out. Polly and Lucy had untied their tent ropes.

"Oh, dear, your tent's fallen down," Polly called, running back across the garden. "Perhaps you'd better go indoors."

Yuck and Little Eric crawled from the bundle of mouldy material. "We'll get them back," Yuck whispered. "Watch this." He took off one of his socks. It was stripy and long. He poked a twig in its end to look like a forked tongue. "**Hissssssssss**," he said. "Let's see how they handle THE SNAKE."

Yuck and Little Eric sneaked to Polly and Lucy's tent. They could hear music coming from inside. Polly had her radio on and Lucy was singing. Yuck poked his sock through the entrance. "**Hissssssssss**."

Inside the tent, Polly tugged Lucy's arm. "What's that sound?" she asked.

"Hissssssssss."

Lucy stopped singing. "It sounds like a—"

"AAARGH!" Polly shrieked, seeing a snake slithering into the tent, its tongue sticking out hissing.

"Hisssssssssssssss."

"Snake!" she cried.

"Help! It's going to bite us!" Lucy screamed. She picked up Polly's radio and whacked the snake on the head.

The radio smashed.

Just then, the tent's zip opened. It was
Dad. "What's going on in here?" he asked.
"A snake's trying to bite us," Lucy said.

Dad looked
down. He
pinched his
nose. "Polly,
Lucy, it's just a
smelly sock."

"A sock?"

Yuck stepped
out from behind the tree. "Oh, there it is,"
he said. "I've been looking everywhere
for that." Yuck grabbed the sock then ran
back with Little Eric. They dived into their
tent laughing.

From the side pocket of the backpack
Yuck took out his book: **How to Survive
in The Wild**. He flicked through the pages
looking at Bushtucker Bill's amazing
expeditions and reading his explorers' tips on
How to Build a Raft, *How to Live in a Volcano*
and even *How to Survive a Bear Attack*.

As Yuck and Little Eric were reading the book, they heard the zip of their tent opening. Polly poked her head through the entrance. "I've come to tell you that you're no longer allowed in our half of the garden," she said, then she marched off smugly.

Yuck and Little Eric looked out. Polly had laid Dad's hosepipe down the middle of the lawn. On the other side of the garden, Lucy was putting up a sign saying **NO EXPLORING ALLOWED**.

Yuck turned to Little Eric. "This calls for specialist equipment," he said.

From the backpack Yuck took out his catapult, then he sneaked to the vegetable patch where Dad was planting seeds.

While Dad had his back turned, Yuck filled the catapult with handfuls of pumpkin seeds. He raced back to Little Eric and they lay by the hosepipe looking across at the enemy camp. They fired the

seeds into the tree above Polly and Lucy's tent, then watched as birds flew to the branches to feed.

Inside their tent, Polly and Lucy were making daisy chains.

"What's that sound?" Lucy asked.

Polly listened. "It sounds like rain."

She poked her head out and saw bird poo plopping down from above. Their pretty tent was splattered with it. "Urgh! Poo!" she cried. A dollop of bird poo landed on Polly's head.

Lucy poked her head out and got plopped on too. "Eyugh! It's sticky!" she yelled, wiping her hair.

"Watch this," Little Eric whispered to Yuck. He ran to the flowerbed where bees were buzzing among the flowers. He picked a flower and took it to Lucy.

"Hey, you're not allowed on our side!" Lucy said.

"But I've come to give you this flower to say sorry," Little Eric told her.

"It's very pretty," Lucy said, surprised.

"It smells nice too. Sniff it."

Lucy put the flower to her nose.

BUZZZZ!

"Aaargh!" she yelled. A bee flew out. "A bee stung by dose!"

Lucy's nose was red and throbbing.

"Oh, dear. That looks sore, Lucy," Little
Eric said. "Perhaps you should go indoors."

Lucy pushed him back to the other side
of the garden. "It's YOU who'll be going
indoors. You'll see!"

All afternoon Polly and Lucy tried to get
rid of Yuck and Little Eric, and Yuck and
Little Eric tried to get rid of Polly and Lucy.

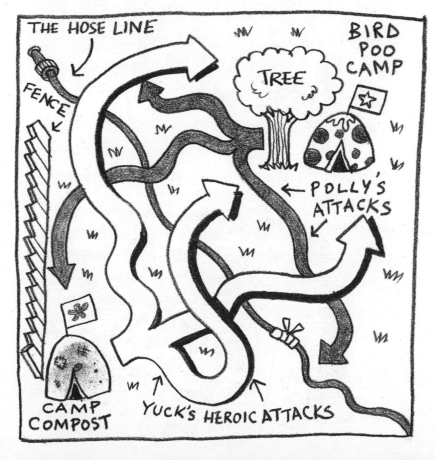

When Yuck and Little Eric were
pretending they were exploring a desert,
Polly turned
on the
hosepipe to
make it rain.

When Polly and Lucy were sunbathing,
Little Eric
swapped
their suntan
lotion for
mayonnaise.

MAYO

When Yuck and Little Eric
were pretending they were
climbing a mountain,
Lucy pelted them with
Dad's tomatoes.

And when Polly and Lucy
were reading magazines
in their tent, Yuck
laid a trail of sugar
to the entrance and
a long line of ants
scurried inside. Polly
ran out screaming:
"Help! There are
ants in my pants!"

At about six o'clock, Mum called from the kitchen: "Dinner's ready." She came to

the back door carrying a plate of hotdogs.

Yuck, Little Eric, Polly and Lucy all rushed up the garden. Yuck and Little Eric scoffed their hotdogs with lashings of ketchup. They watched as Polly and Lucy put theirs onto paper plates to have as a picnic.

Yuck had a brilliant idea – a way to finally get Polly and Lucy to go back indoors. "Wouldn't it be scary if a big wild animal was to come and eat Polly and Lucy's food?" he whispered to Little Eric.

Quickly, Yuck ran to his tent and fetched his fishing rod from the pile of survival equipment. He'd made it himself from a wooden cane, a length of string and a bent pin. He sneaked across the garden with Little Eric and climbed the tree by Polly and Lucy's tent.

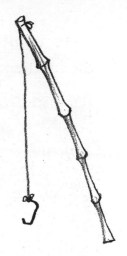

Yuck snapped two twigs from the tree and handed them to Little Eric. "When Polly and Lucy sit down, throw a twig into the bushes."

As Polly and Lucy sat on their blanket to begin their picnic, Little Eric threw one of the twigs into the bushes. Polly and Lucy both looked round.

"What was that noise?" Lucy asked.

Yuck lowered
his fishing line. The
bent pin hooked
the sausage from
Polly's hotdog
and he quickly
pulled it up.

Polly turned
back round. "Hey!
Where's my
sausage gone?" she
cried. She glared
at Lucy. "Did you
steal my sausage?"

"It wasn't me,"
Lucy said.

Yuck and Little
Eric giggled.

"Now," Yuck whispered again.

Little Eric threw the other twig into the bushes.

"Listen," Lucy said. "I heard it again. There's something moving in the bushes."

As Polly and Lucy looked round, Yuck lowered his fishing line again. The bent pin hooked the sausage from Lucy's hotdog and he quickly pulled it back up.

"What if it was an animal?" Lucy said, turning back round. "Hey! My sausage has gone too!" She glared at Polly. "Did you steal my sausage?"

"It wasn't me," Polly said.

As Polly and Lucy started arguing, Yuck and Little Eric scoffed the sausages then climbed down from the tree.

"What's the matter with you two?"
Yuck asked.

"Lucy stole my sausage," Polly said.

"No. Polly stole MY sausage," Lucy said.

"Maybe an animal ate them," Yuck said.

Polly and Lucy looked at Yuck, puzzled.

"An animal?" Lucy asked.

"What animal?" Polly asked.

"A WILD animal!" Yuck told them,
glancing to the bushes.

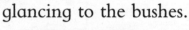

"A really wild,
sausage-eating animal,"
Little Eric added.

"It was probably
something dangerous,"
Yuck said. "Like a bear!"

"A bear!" Lucy cried, glancing around
nervously.

"Don't be silly," Polly said. " There aren't
bears in the garden."

"I'd be careful if I were you," Yuck told
them. "If a hungry bear's around here, then
it might come back tonight to eat YOU."

Lucy looked up at the sky. It was starting to get dark. "I don't want to be eaten by a bear," she whimpered.

Yuck and Little Eric strolled back to their tent giggling.

"Do you think they fell for it?" Little Eric whispered.

"If not, they soon will," Yuck replied.

As night fell, Yuck took a torch from his backpack and put on the Hairy-Bear Beast Glove. He crept to the flowerbed and made big paw-prints in the mud as if a bear had been there.

Little Eric crept to the tree by Polly and Lucy's tent. While they were inside, he took a stick and scratched claw marks into the tree trunk. Then Yuck and Little Eric hid in the bushes.

"**GRRRR**," Yuck said.

"**GRRRR**," Little Eric said.

In the tent, Polly and Lucy were opening their midnight feast – a big bag of marshmallows.

"What that's noise?" Lucy asked. "It sounded like an animal growling."

"It's probably just a squirrel," Polly said.

"But squirrels don't growl."

Polly unzipped the tent and shone her torch outside.

"**GRRRR**," she heard from the bushes.

"I don't like this," Lucy said nervously.

Yuck and Little Eric quietly crawled behind the tree. Yuck stuffed the Hairy-Bear Beast Glove up his T-shirt, and they stepped out.

Polly shone her torch on them. "What are you two doing here?" she asked.

"We've come to warn you," Yuck replied. "We just saw a bear."

"Nonsense. There aren't bears in the garden."

"Yes there are. We saw a big one sniffing around your tent."

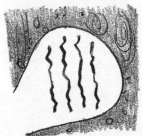

"It was sharpening its claws on this tree," Little Eric said.

Polly shone her torch to the tree and saw the claw marks on it.

"It tramped across the flowerbed," Yuck said.

Polly shone her torch to the flowerbed and saw the paw-prints in the mud.

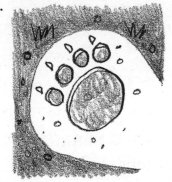

Lucy reached from the tent and tugged on Polly's ankle. She was trembling. "Bears are dangerous, Polly," she said.

Polly looked at Yuck suspiciously. She shone her torch into his eyes, trying to see if he was lying. "If there's really a bear in the garden, how come you're not afraid?"

"Because we're explorers," Yuck told her. "Explorers aren't afraid of anything."

"You'd better not be up to something," Polly said, and she ducked back into the tent to find Lucy.

"I'm scared," Lucy said. "Let's go indoors."

"But it doesn't make sense," Polly told her, popping a marshmallow into her mouth. "Bears don't live in the garden. Yuck's just trying to scare us."

At that moment, something started scratching on the side of their tent.

"Listen!" Lucy whispered.

It sounded like claws.

"**GRRRR**... **GRRRR**," they heard.

"It's right outside," Lucy said. "It's coming to get us!"

They saw the tent's zip moving upwards. A clawed hairy hand reached inside!

Then they heard a voice. "Get back, bear! Shoo!" it said. It sounded like Yuck.

Suddenly the clawed hand vanished and the growls stopped. The zip on the tent opened and Yuck peered inside. "It's okay. I scared it off," he said.

Polly and Lucy were both trembling.

"You scared off a bear? How?" Polly asked.

"It was easy," Yuck replied. Tucked into his trousers was his book **How to Survive in The Wild**. He pulled it out and showed it to them. "This book could save your life. It shows how to scare off a bear, how to wrestle a bear and even how to trap a bear too. What a pity you've not read it."

Yuck pointed at Polly and Lucy's bag of marshmallows. "The bear was probably

after those," he said. "You should give them to me to look after, then go indoors where it's safe."

Polly clutched the marshmallows tightly. "I'm not giving you these. These are our midnight feast."

"Well don't blame me if the bear comes back," Yuck said. He zipped up the tent then walked off giggling.

Polly and Lucy huddled together.

"I don't want to get eaten," Lucy said. "Please can we go indoors?"

"Wait a second," Polly told her. "Look at this." She was shining her torch at a book by her side. It was Yuck's book. "He must have accidentally left it behind," she whispered. It was open on a page headed *How To Make a Bear Trap*.

There was a picture of a net with a rope attached to it. "I've got an idea," Polly said sniggering. "If we can trap that bear, we could set it loose on Yuck and Little Eric!"

"That would get rid of them once and for all," Lucy said.

Polly unzipped the tent. "Come on."

"Where are you going?" Lucy asked.

"We need a net," Polly told her.

Under the cover of darkness, Polly and
Lucy tiptoed to Yuck and Little Eric's tent.
They could hear snoring.

"Yuck's got a net in his survival
equipment," Polly whispered. She unzipped
the tent and saw Yuck and Little Eric in
their sleeping bags with their eyes closed.

Their survival
equipment was by
Yuck's feet. Polly
reached in and
dragged out the
net and rope.

"Nicely done," Lucy said, and they
crept back across the garden to prepare
the bear trap.

Yuck and Little Eric opened their eyes.

"They fell
for it," Little
Eric whispered.

"This is going
to be fun,"
Yuck giggled.

Yuck and Little Eric peered out of their tent and saw Lucy shining a torch while Polly set up the bear trap. They watched as Polly laid the net on the ground by the tree, and attached the rope to it. She threw the rope over a branch then dragged its end into her tent. Lucy placed a handful of marshmallows on the ground as bait, then dashed inside after Polly.

Yuck and Little Eric sneaked up the garden. They went indoors to find Mum.

"Hi, Mum," Yuck said.

"What's the matter? Can't you two sleep?" Mum asked.

"We're thirsty," Yuck told her. "Please could we have a glass of milk?"

"Of course you can," Mum said. She took a carton of milk from the fridge and poured Yuck and Little Eric a glass each.

"Polly and Lucy would like some too," Yuck said.

"Can't they sleep either?"

"They asked if you'd take it out to them. They're tucked up in their sleeping bags."

Mum poured two more glasses of milk and carried them outside.

Polly and Lucy were huddled in their tent clutching the end of the rope. "Listen," Polly whispered. "I can hear something."

Footsteps were coming down the garden.

"It's the bear," Lucy said, excitedly.

"Get ready," Polly told her.

They both gripped the rope tightly.

The footsteps stopped outside the front of their tent.

"Now!" Polly said.

They both pulled hard on the rope. There was a *WHOOSH* as the net shot upwards, then an "AARGH!"

"We've got it!" Polly said triumphantly. She leapt from the tent and shone her torch…

"M–m–mum?"

Swinging in the net was Mum. She was covered with milk! "Polly! What on earth do you think you're doing?" she shrieked.

"I-I-I thought you were a bear," Polly said surprised.

"A bear? Don't be ridiculous! Get me down from here this instant!"

Polly let go of the rope and the net dropped to the ground. Mum threw it off and stood up wiping milk from her face. "Polly, Lucy, you're to come inside at once!" she said crossly.

"But Mum—"

"That's the last time you two go camping in the garden!"

As Mum dragged Polly and Lucy towards the house, they passed Yuck and Little Eric running the other way.

Yuck was wearing the Hairy-Bear Beast Glove. He gave Polly a wave.

"It was you, Yuck!" Polly said angrily. "YOU were the bear! I HATE you!"

"**GRRRR**... Goodnight," Yuck said giggling.

Little Eric ran to Polly and Lucy's tent and picked up the marshmallows from the ground. "Look, Yuck! Food rations!" he called.

Yuck and Little Eric scoffed the marshmallows, then both raised their hands making the sign of THE CLAW.

"**GRRRR.** It's great to be in the wild!"